MURDER AT JAX BEACH

A HARPER ROGERS COZY MYSTERY

SHARON E. BUCK

D1520399

SOUTHERN CHICK LIT

For more information, or to book an event, contact : sharon@sharonebuck.com

http://www.SharonEBuck.com

To join my VIP Newsletter and to receive a **FREE** book, go to

Cover design by Steven Novak, NovakIllustration.com

First Edition: March 2024

CONTENTS

CHAPTER 1

There was a surfer sitting on the edge of the ocean watching the waves. His board was next to him.

Only problem was he was dead. Well, he looked dead. Maybe he was just sleeping, and my imagination was playing tricks on me. That happens sometimes.

I had gone to Jacksonville Beach aka Jax Beach because I needed some alone time to think. My life was messed up and I figured the salty ocean air would help to clear my mind. Hopefully, add some sanity to it.

Finding a sitting-up dead body wasn't exactly what I expected to find at six a.m. on a hot, humid summer morning. Yeah, saying hot and humid in Florida is a little redundant since that's the way it is three hundred sixty-four and a half days in the year.

What made me think the surfer dude was dead? There was red stuff leaking from the back of his head down the back of his wet suit.

I looked around trying to see if there was anyone close by. Except for the seagulls darting about in the air and swooping down to land on the wet Florida sand, it was just me and the dead guy.

My idea of a tranquil morning walk dissipated faster than the sun was rising over the Atlantic Ocean.

I kind of wondered if the blond-haired guy was really dead as I walked a little closer to him.

"Hey!" I shouted. Nothing. "Hey!"

Easing up on his left side, I said, "Hey, buddy, you okay?"

That's when I saw the devastation caused by the hole in the back of his head. His face was gone. I hurled everything I had eaten in the past twenty-four hours. I have a notoriously weak stomach to begin with but seeing no face first thing in the morning...before coffee...was beyond unnerving.

My hands were shaking as I punched nine-one-one.

"What's your emergency?"

"Um, I, um, there's a dead guy on the beach."

"Which beach?"

"Jax Beach, just down from the pier."

After asking several more questions and, I'm sure dispatch was trying to keep me on the line and not run away, two beach guards came roaring up on their little four-wheel sand motorcycles. They got off and approached me cautiously. Their hands out to the side. I could see what appeared to be tasers but I couldn't tell if they were actually armed or not.

I turned and threw up in the ocean this time. Probably wasn't a wise thing to do with the incoming tide but at least it was in the ocean and not on the sand.

"What's going on here?"

My brain had already gone into massive overload. I wanted to ask him if he was a special kind of stupid but decided that might not bode well for me.

"Um, um, I was walking and saw this guy and, um, um..." I turned and hurled again into the ocean.

If I'm going to throw up, I'd rather do it in the privacy of my apartment and not in a public place, much less in front of guys who were about my age. This was beyond embarrassing.

My brain shut down, everything zoomed into a narrow tunnel. I was desperately trying to make sure I wasn't throwing up on myself. When I finally looked up there were police officers from the Jax Beach Police Department everywhere. They were all standing a healthy distance from me. The good news is no one was laughing at me and my situation. I'm guessing they've all seen this before during spring break and the summertime with the hundreds of over-indulging young people.

Squinting my eyes shut and taking a deep breath trying to quell the nausea, it occurred to me that a throwing up female must pose a serious threat to them since they were all standing about eight feet or so from me. The only weapon I had was whatever was spewing out of my mouth into the ocean. Yeah, big threat.

"Ma'am, do you have anything on your person we need to know about?" This was from a slim, reasonably attractive female officer. Shaking my head, she came over next to me. "You, okay?"

"No. There's a dead guy with no face." I was finally able to stand up straight and look at her. "How can a dead guy be sitting up?"

She ignored my question. "Is there someone you want to call?"

Even with the overwhelm of seeing a dead guy first thing in the morning, my brain was swimming up and down but not in a straight line. It was bobbing like a cork on the ocean waves.

"What? Are you arresting me?" my voice had gone up several notches.

"No. You look like you're in shock and I wanted to know if you needed a friend to come be with you."

The only person I could think of was Sam Needles, a Palm Park detective I had sort of become friendly with over the past several months.

My brain was screaming at me that I had friends in Jacksonville. It made more sense for me to call one of them instead of Sam. I don't know why I thought of Sam first. Maybe because he was a police officer, and I thought any little bit of law enforcement help would me.

"Um, do you know Detective Sam Needles in Palm Park? He, um, might come."

The female officer rocked back a little on her heels. She semi-smiled. "Sam Needles? Black hair, cute dimples?"

I nodded while my mind was frantically trying to figure out if this officer and Sam had dated or were a couple or what? All of that based on a simple smile.

Meanwhile, I was mentally slapping myself silly. Why was the only person I could think of calling was another police officer in another county an hour away? It's not like I didn't have friends here in Jacksonville. They just weren't the kind you'd invite to a death-on-the-beach party. My brain was shutting down. I was re-evaluating my life once again.

"Um, what did you say? I think my brain rode out on one of the waves." I was trying to be funny which went over like a lead balloon. She wasn't smiling, just standing there looking at me. She probably looked at dead fish bait like this, impassive.

"I said do you have his phone number?"

I handed her my phone. "He's in there somewhere."

I never handed my phone over to anyone. Why do it now? Everything seemed to speed up and then slow down. It wasn't from the fresh salt air whipping around my face. I was having too much external stimuli with seeing the dead guy.

Watching her do a mental eye roll, I'm sure she probably thought I had lost my marbles or was mentally ill or just a female whacko on the beach.

I watched as the police officers were cordoning off the area with the dead guy. One guy was busy snapping pictures from different angles like a person on speed. The minions from a local funeral home showed up in a brand-new white minivan with the funeral home's name prominently displayed on the side. If caterers can promote themselves and their restaurants, there's no reason why a funeral home shouldn't be able to do the same thing, I thought. Although, admittedly, it was probably in poor taste.

She had found Sam's name, spoke to him for a moment, and handed me the phone.

"Another dead body and you called me?" His voice sounded slightly amused.

"How did you ever survive the first thirty years of your life?"

Okay, that was just wrong...and maybe that's what I needed to shake the cobwebs from my brain. Anger can do that to a person.

"You know perfectly well, I'm only twenty-eight and you're..."

He laughed. "I know how old I am. I also know how old you are. The question is what happened?"

I quickly explained what I had seen. The lady police officer was paying close attention to my explanation. I ended with, "For whatever reason, the only person I could think to call was you."

There was an amused semi-snort on the other end of the line. I could tell Sam was struggling not to laugh. "Do tell. Okay, tell Cherise I'll be there in about thirty minutes. I actually happen to be at Town Center."

I was annoyed. Why? Well, I couldn't really explain it and now was not the time to overanalyze every aspect of my life, which, unfortunately, I was prone to do on a daily basis. Analysis paralysis is what the so-called psychobabble gurus call it. I prefer to call it a creative use of overindulging my brain cells in a time vacuum.

"Is your name Cherise?" Well, that was just stupid on my part. She was the only female on the beach besides me.

She nodded, brushing her hair off her forehead. I could see little beads of sweat forming along her hairline. Humidity rarely, if ever, leaves Florida weather regardless of where you are in the state.

"Sam said to tell you he'd be here in thirty minutes or less."

"Did you know the deceased?" an officer wearing cargo police shorts and a short-sleeved shirt walked up and asked me.

"No."

Cherise proceeded to give him the rundown on what I had said over the phone to Sam.

I know it's Florida, I know it's always hot and humid, I was sweating profusely, it wasn't even seven a.m., but these cops were working at the speed of a turtle laying eggs. They were sloooow.

They didn't seem to be particularly interested in doing much of anything. Most of them seem to be just standing around and shooting the breeze with each other. Our precious city government dollars at work.

I spotted Sam ambling over the sugar sand dune and coming down to the hard-packed beach sand. He was carrying three cups of coffee. He handed one to Cherise, gave her a lazy smile, and a much bigger smile to me as he gave me the coffee. "I figured you both could use one."

Cherise thanked him and went over to the group of men just standing around and appearing to be doing nothing. Perhaps they were thinking, there wasn't any physical motion needed for that.

Maybe they were solving the case. They were just watching the coroner lift the body up into the gurney.

I started to ask Sam a question, but he held up a finger. "Drink the coffee, Harper. Let me see what the guys have to say."

My hand was shaking so badly that if the cup had not had a lid on it nothing would be left in the Styrofoam container.

Watching Sam out of the corner of my eye, I was still trying to process everything going on. My nerves could have ridden a pogo stick as much bouncing up and down they were doing.

Walking back over to me, he asked, "Harper, you know who that is, don't you?"

I frowned and shook my head sipping my coffee.

"They think that it's Mickey Rogers' son Mason."

CHAPTER 2

Shocked **I didn't know what** to say. There was empty space floating around in my brain. I know the old saying that nature abhors a vacuum didn't seem to be true in my case. There was air in my noggin. No dots were being connected; no straight lines were aligning with anything. It felt like my very being was a black hole in the universe where things disappeared forever.

I hadn't heard the name Mickey Rogers in years, and it took a moment for it to connect.

"You, they, think it's who?" I finally managed to stutter out. Then I turned and threw up in the ocean again.

How did this happen? This was my biological father's son? I didn't know he had any children.

My dad had divorced my mother when I was two and rode off into the sunset to God knows where. I had never seen or talked to the man since he walked out the door.

My thoughts resembled a jumbled labyrinth of knotted strings. I vaguely wondered if my mother knew what became of him. It was always possible.

My mother had told me several times when I was little that she and Mickey, I'm not calling him Dad since I never knew him, had had a major disagreement on my name when I was born. She said they'd had a lot of arguments before Mickey took off for good.

My name is Harper Elizabeth Rogers. Yes, my initials spell HER. She thought it was funny, and it was a lot better than Mickey's name choice of Harper Olivia Rogers aka HOR. Mom was adamant that her daughter's initials would not be compared to a lowly, jail-prone street walker. She won in the end.

Mom, however, wasn't amused when I told her I was going to be a novelist. "Just because I named you Harper doesn't mean you have to be a writer like Harper Lee," she sniffed. "I simply liked the name Harper."

Sadly, she died a couple of years ago before I had graduated from eating peanut butter and jelly sandwiches on a daily basis to eating out at decent restaurants several times a week. I like to think she would have been proud of me and my career choice.

It suddenly occurred to me why would Sam know that I was related to Mickey Rogers.

"Sam," I almost dreaded asking him, afraid of his answer, "how did you know Mickey Rogers is my biological father?"

I wanted to be excessively clear that I didn't know the man except by name only. He was simply a sperm donor as far as I was concerned. I hadn't thought about him in years and, honestly, I wouldn't recognize him if he were standing in front of me.

"He told me."

Oh, the day just keeps getting better and better. Then it occurred to me, why did the cops know Mickey Rogers and his son? And, more importantly, how was this connected to me? I don't like it when murders happen around me, it makes me nervous for a variety of reasons.

"Why?"

"Why what, Harper?" Sam had a slight smile on his face while tilting his head.

I groaned. Sam and I had flirted slightly several months ago. Yes, we have gone out several times since then but nothing serious. I was still trying to overcome the devastating effects from my divorce. I simply wasn't interested in a relation-ship. Well, platonic but nothing more.

"He's a decent musician and a lousy comedian. His comedic timing is atrocious."

I just stood there, blinking my eyes, trying to absorb this information about someone who was technically related to me but also someone I knew absolutely nothing about.

"He plays guitar in a cover band that periodically blasts through Jacksonville. I met him when," he nodded his head at Cherise, "she and I dated for a brief moment in time."

Score one for me. As a woman, we have the sixth sense in spades when it comes to knowing if another female has dated someone. Must be some type of pheromones that only we can detect.

"You had just come out with your book Bowling and Murder and were on Good Morning, America."

I smiled. That one morning show had taken me from eating very frugally to where I could eat out all the time and not have to stress about the cost.

Sam smiled and continued, "Cherise and I met him backstage at a meet-and-greet. He had asked where we were from. She said Jacksonville and I said Palm Park. He asked if I knew you. Well, I knew who you were and that you had grown up in Palm Park, but I didn't really know you. So, I said no. He said you were a very famous author, and that he was your dad. The line needed to keep moving, he turned, and started talking to someone else. That was it."

I almost couldn't breathe. Mickey Rogers actually knew who I was? I wondered why he had never bothered to contact me, especially after my mother had died.

"Sam, why would I know Mason Rogers? I didn't even know I had a half-brother until just now. In fact, I didn't even know Mickey was still alive. I'm still in shock from finding that out."

"Because there was a note in Mason's hand that said, 'If I'm dead, find Harper Rogers'."

I fainted.

CHAPTER 3

Just call me wimpy. I am a writer. I don't go to the gym, I don't have Pilates muscles, I hide behind a computer and spew words out that, hopefully, people like to read. My fingers are exercised a lot every time the sun passes go. In general, if I jump up too quickly from a strenuous workout on the keyboard, I can become swimmy-headed. Finding out that a murdered man was basically accusing me of causing his death caused all my body's blood flow to head south to my toes. It was a sheer wonder that

I didn't have seriously fat feet when I regained consciousness.

I heard voices but they were distant and, quite honestly, I didn't feel like opening my eyes. I was comfortable with my eyes shut. I was probably going to be arrested for murder. I wondered if I was allowed to write in jail. I was sure I wasn't going to look good in orange or whatever the color du jour was for prison uniforms. I didn't want to have to learn karate to protect myself inside government-issue human cages from people I would never ever have coffee with in real life. My brain felt like a dysfunctional marriage of Legos and Tinker Toys, nothing was matching up nor did it want to. Weird thoughts were running through my head at the speed of Einstein's theory of relativity. Maybe I had inhaled a cosmic ray of energy. I took a deep breath.

"Harper, I saw your eyelids twitch. Open them," ordered Sam. He was interrupting some seriously good non-productive thoughts.

Sighing deeply to let him know how annoyed I was, I opened them and then slowly sat up.

"Am I being arrested?" I timidly asked. I was searching frantically in my brain if I knew any attorneys I could call to get me out of jail. None came to mind. Well, that's not exactly true. I did know one, but I wasn't exactly sure if he'd represent me since he overheard me saying at a social function that he only handled schoolboard clients and they couldn't fire him regardless of the advice he gave them. Probably not the right thing to say at a public schoolboard meeting. I had tried to tell him I meant it as a joke. I don't think he has a sense of humor but, to be fair, I'm not wild about hearing someone criticize my writing either. Maybe he'd just attribute that unfortunate remark to my having a glass of wine that evening. I probably should never admit to him that I was only holding it and not drinking it.

"No, you're not being arrested," replied Cherise. Sweat was running in a straight line down the sides of her face, "but you do need to give me your statement again."

I arched my eyebrows. "How many times do I need to do that?"

"Until we're satisfied you're not lying."

Cherise wasn't smiling when she said that. I was not going to vote for her as a pseudo–Miss Congeniality. Errant thoughts were darting through my brain trying to piece together what was going on.

"Is Mickey here in the area?"

Sam and Cherise looked at each other and shrugged. One of the other officers gestured for them to come join their group.

I watched as they all turned and stared at the condo building behind the sand dunes. One of the officers pointed at it. I couldn't tell what floor he was pointing at, but it suddenly occurred to me I was in the clear. If they were pointing at the building, that meant someone had shot Mason. It also meant that someone probably had a high-powered rifle to shoot from that distance. I don't know much about guns, but I surmised a guess that whoever used the rifle, they were probably military or ex-military. I did know shotguns and handguns couldn't hit anything accurately from that far away. Was this a paid hit? What was going on? This was much more than just a random, theoretically accidental, homicide. And why, oh, why was my half-brother holding a note with my name on it? As far as I knew, I had never even seen him before. I certainly didn't know him.

"You can leave, Harper. We have all of your information and I'm sure someone will be in touch with you." Cherise held out her hand to pull me into an upright standing position.

Sam had his hands on his hips. "You going to finish your walk?"

"Wait!" I held up my hand. "This isn't making any sense. Why were you guys pointing at the condo?"

Then my sheer nosiness came alive and I blurted out, "Why were you at Town Center so early in the day? None of the stores open until ten a.m."

"Checking things out." Sam was very nonchalant. Realistically, it was a nunya – none of my business. I was trying to justify my nosiness as info for one of my new books I was yet to write.

One of the officers walked past us when Sam said just loud enough for him to hear, "Yes, I'll walk with you. I'll be your personal bodyguard."

Part of me wanted to believe it was his way of flirting, the other part of me was highly annoyed that he was posturing for another officer.

"It's a free country. You can walk wherever you want to," I snapped. Also, I was loud enough for the officer to hear. Childish? Yes, of course. Did it make me feel better? Absolutely it did.

Sam merely frowned, nodded his head up and to the right, "You walking or what?"

Gritting my teeth and finally giving up as we turned to walk side by side down the beach. "Why'd you say that to the cops?"

He grinned, showing off his dimple in his right cheek. "Do I have to have a reason? Come on, Harper, you really do need to walk with me."

It suddenly dawned on me, I'm blaming my mental slowness on all the unwelcome events of the morning, that Sam had information he was going to share with me.

"Yeah, sure," I said begrudgingly and started to walk.

As soon as we got out of ear range of the beach cops, Sam turned his head toward me. "We're pretty sure someone on the sixth floor of the condo shot Mason."

I was so pleased with myself for guessing that that I blurted out, "It had to be a high-powered rifle and someone with a military background, right?"

Sam did a side-eye glance at me. "You might not want to share that information. That puts you back in the category of knowing too much but, yes, you are correct. Mason was hit in the middle of his head. That means someone had to calculate wind velocity, wind direction, altitude, elevation, range to the target, ambient temperature..."

"In other words, the sniper was a pro and had to know what he was doing." I was so proud of myself.

Sam just nodded his head. "Yep. The question is why?"

"Um, that also means one of the cops knows about wind elevation, etc., right?"

Sam laughed, "Do you have any idea how many cops are ex-military? Any of them could have come up with the same solution."

I was walking in the ocean and Sam was a couple of feet away. He had on sneakers, and I was walking with just my bare-naked toes and feet in the coolish water. The water in Florida doesn't really get cold until January and then it only stays cold for about six to eight weeks. The temperature during the summer-time averages about eighty-three de-grees. The Gulf of Mexico, on the oth-er hand aka the west coast of Florida, averages about eighty-eight degrees. I personally don't care for the west coast of Florida. The Gulf is like warm bathwa-ter as far as I was concerned...and there were no waves. I've made more waves in a bathtub than you ever see on the Gulf unless there is a huge hurricane rolling in. It's boring.

The Atlantic Ocean by Jacksonville has a lot of waves, there are plenty of surfers. I seriously doubt most of them could surf

California waves but it's still fun to watch them.

They were now starting to show up and paddling out to catch the swells. As hot and humid as it already was, the day was promising to be a scorcher, it was still only about nine in the morning.

"Why are you out walking so early, Harper?" Sam had small rivers of sweat running down both sides of his face. Let me point out that it's no longer called perspiration when that occurs. It's just pure out-and-out sweat. He was wiping the sweat off his face about every ten seconds. Yes, I counted because I was trying very hard not to do the same thing myself. I like air conditioning...a lot. I don't exercise in a gym because I don't like to sweat. I try to convince myself typing on a keyboard at a furious pace counts as exercise...with no sweat.

When I first started walking this morning I wasn't sweating. My original plan had been to walk on the beach, feel the sand between my toes, get my feet wet, and then head back home. I just wanted to walk and think for about thirty minutes. Finding Mason dead disrupted my entire morning and messed up my entire thinking process. How could one possibly think after stumbling upon a dead body? My thoughts were just going to have to continue to swirl in outer space with no destination.

"Are you even listening to me?" asked Sam wiping the sweat off his face, he sounded annoyed. He glanced over at me.

"Um," I was frantically trying to remember what he had said. "Um, why?"

Sam glanced over at me. This time he was visibly annoyed. "What do you have in common with Mason, your biological dad, and a sniper?"

I shrugged, thinking, "Nothing that I'm aware of."

"Harper, when was the last time you saw your dad?"

I didn't remember. I couldn't even pull up a memory of what he looked like. The man could have been standing in front of me and I wouldn't have been able to pick him out of a lineup.

It's weird how childhood feelings suddenly surface. They're not logical and, most probably, aren't even true except for what we believe about them. Maybe I screamed too loud as a two-year-old toddler. Maybe I didn't hug him enough. Who knows? All I knew was he was there one day and then he was gone. As far as I knew, I hadn't laid eyes on him in twenty-six years or so.

I shrugged. "I don't know. Maybe when I was two. Mom said he left and never returned."

"Any pictures of him or of the two of you together?"

Shaking my head no, "Why? You've seen him more than I have. Why would you need a picture?"

"Just curious." Sam kept his eyes focused straight ahead.

"Do you know something you're not sharing with me?" Rather than being aggravated, I was actually more curious. His line of questioning indicated to me that he knew something he wasn't willing to tell me.

We were almost back to where police personnel were still taking pictures and measurements.

Patience isn't one of my strong suits. "Well?" I tried to sound demanding, but it came out more like Alvin from Alvin and the Chipmunks. I cleared my throat and tried again. "Well?"

"It's a deep subject." He chuckled. "Harper, catch you later."

I just stood there trying to figure out what was going on. Nothing came to mind.

Cherise ambled over to me. "Harper, I'm sure we'll have some more questions for you at some point, but you can leave now."

"I have a question."

She turned. "Yes?"

"What do you think is going on?"

Poker-faced, she answered, "Police business, Harper, police business."

Weirdness is the only thing I could think of on the way back to my car. Walking up to the side of my car, I could see there was a note on my windshield. I grinned, maybe Sam wanted to meet for coffee or lunch but didn't want to ask me in front of Cherise or the other police officers.

Picking up the note from under the wipers, I flipped it open.

"You're next."

CHAPTER 4

That's not good. I turned and ran back down to the beach. I didn't see Sam anywhere, but I did see Cherise. I waved at her trying to get her attention. She spotted me but didn't wave back. I still wasn't going to vote for her as Miss Congeniality.

Huffing and puffing as I ran up to her, I hate running, I handed her the note. She glanced at it. "You know you should consider working out."

I snorted and tried to take a deep breath at the same time. "This was under my windshield wiper blade," I finally managed to say. Trying to find a spark of wit to craft a clever retort to her snide remark about my exercise habits, nothing fired in my brain cylinders at that moment. My most clever remarks often happen several hours later when I've had a chance to think about such things.

She barely looked at it and handed it back to me. "So?"

My nerves were frayed, they were not going to be put back together with disinterest, glue, or even chocolate. "What do you mean so?" I shouted. Pointing at some of the police techs, "Get one of them to dust it for fingerprints. Maybe it's from the killer, I don't know but DO

SOMETHING!" My voice continued to rise until I was almost screaming at her.

The other officers were paying a lot more attention to me than what I probably deserved but, then again, in their line of work, they need to be aware at all times.

One of them started to walk over, Cherise waved him back. "I've got it."

Sneering, I snapped, "Got what? You haven't got anything, and you don't seem to be much interested in solving a murder and now a threat on my life."

"Miss Rogers, that note could mean anything and it may not have even been meant for you."

"You don't know that." I was livid. "It was on my car. Under my wipers. It says you're next. Just what exactly do you think that means, Miss Police Officer?"

Probably not the wisest thing to do is to antagonize a police officer while they're investigating an open murder case where you might be the prime suspect.

In my excitement or lunacy, I must have inadvertently invaded her personal territory because she held up her hand in the universal stop motion.

"Miss Rogers, you need to back up a few feet. We are investigating an active murder scene. We appreciate your cooperation and understand why you are upset. However, that note could have been left on your car accidentally. It may have been a practical joke..."

I held up my hand. She ignored it.

"That same note may be on several other cars. But you need to leave so we can do our job. Again, we appreciate your cooperation."

Great. She's not remotely interested. I wonder if Sam thinks anything about it, but I don't know where he's disappeared to or even what he's doing. He did say this was his day off. I probably shouldn't bother him for the rest of the day then. I think I am already blurring the boundary lines on personal versus professional time.

In my world, I ignore those boundary lines. I mean I do pay attention to the professional ones...most of the time. But a lot of my work as a writer involves research and creativity, therefore, those lines often overlap. Plus, I really don't care about crossing so-called boundary lines. If someone's a friend, I don't think anything about asking them about their job if it helps me with a plot or a character. Even if I don't know you as a friend, I still don't think anything about asking questions.

I was feeling thwarted by Cherise's lack of interest. I stomped off and left to go home. So much for my morning beach walk, clearing the cobwebs from my brain, and solving the world's problems.

Deciding I needed to do some research on dear old dad while driving back to Palm Park, I thought about googling him. Since Mom was no longer in the land of the living, I couldn't very well ask her. Mom had been an only child, so I didn't have any aunts, uncles, or cousins to ask. I couldn't recall us ever going to a relative's house for vacation or any holiday gatherings.

You might think we'd be like sisters or close friends. You'd be wrong. Surprisingly, Mom and I weren't really that close. She did her thing and I did mine. We saw each other at breakfast and dinner and that was it; otherwise, I was in school all day.

As a kid, it probably never occurred to me to ask questions about family. I could be obtuse at times. As an adult, I guess I simply didn't care. I often wore blinders and could be somewhat oblivious to many things that others took for granted.

I wasn't remotely interested in the 'Find Your DNA Match' websites. If I hadn't heard from someone in twenty years, I couldn't imagine why we needed to start communicating now. I could care less if there were so-called skeletons in the closet from a hundred years ago. It certainly wasn't going to do me any good now.

Musing about dear old dad, maybe I should see what the internet had to say about him.

He was a musician, just like Sam said. He did have a website. No mention of a son or daughter. It also didn't mention where he was based. He could live in Nome, Alaska for all I knew. Watching a couple of YouTube videos of him playing, I could understand why he played in bar cover bands. He was good, he just wasn't great. There didn't seem to be anything really special about his playing or singing.

Looking in the bathroom mirror while glancing at his website photo on my phone, I really didn't see any family resemblance. I guess that was a good thing because I didn't really have any impetus to continue searching for images.

An unknown number popped up on my phone. Since that was normally Sam, I answered the phone chirpily. "Are you calling for a coffee date?"

There was a slight pause before a robot-sounding voice answered. "Back off before you get hurt." The call was disconnected.

Pulling the phone away from my ear, I just stared at it for a few minutes.

This wasn't good.

CHAPTER 5

Punching in my friend Ronnie's number, I was hoping he'd answer quickly.

"Hello, honey. How you doing today?"

Ronnie was the flamboyant local pet store owner and we had been friends since high school. He welcomed me with open arms when I moved back to Palm Park from Jacksonville after a disastrous failed marriage.

I quickly told him everything going on and ending with, "Ronnie, did you know my dad?"

I could almost see him shaking his head. "No. I don't even remember Mama and Papa ever talking about him growing up. Have you talked to Sam about this? After all, he's a detective."

Almost a semi-snort, I answered, "He said he was at Town Center this morning and it was his day off. I asked him why he was there so early in the morning, and he never answered the question."

Ronnie laughed. "That's a nunya, Harper. It ain't none o' yor business. He might have been having breakfast with someone."

True, there were a ton of fast food and early-morning restaurants in that area.

Maybe I had interrupted a date...a date that went from last night into this morning. A flickering of an emotion I did not understand or could really identify popped up in my brain. Maybe it was jealousy, maybe not. I didn't understand any of these emotions I was experiencing.

Was this a feeling of rejection? Maybe but Sam and I weren't dating. We did meet up for coffee periodically and did go to dinner once in a blue moon but none of those social interactions would constitute a date in my world. We flirted...sort of, maybe. I really wasn't ready to date, I was recovering from my divorce. At least, that's what I was telling myself. I felt like I was in an emotional vacuum and that was okay. I was trudging through life, that I could do because I had been doing it for years. I didn't need emotions. That was a lie. Deep inside I knew I did but I wasn't ready to confront or acknowledge them.

The thought did occur to me that I probably needed to get out more, see other people, make new friends, and not live in my head so much. I tried to justify that thought process by saying I was a writer, and I could live in my head as much as I wanted. I could play make-believe as much as I desired. After all, it's what makes great stories.

I tried justifying my reluctance to engage with others outside of my head. Then I tried to blame my lack of a robust social life on the death of my friend several months ago when we were meeting for a coffee date. I had to be honest, while

Sarah's death was very upsetting, it had nothing to do with this funk I was in. I was already living in my head too much.

All these thoughts flitted through my brain at the speed of an adrenaline junkie as Ronnie was talking.

"Harper, honey, come on down to the store and I'll let you hold some puppies. They'll make you feel better."

I nodded and then realized Ronnie couldn't see me do that. "Yes, okay. Do you want me to pick up a butter pecan coffee for you?"

Ronnie almost squealed with delight. "Harper Elizabeth Rogers, if you do that, I'll love you to the moon and back."

With someone that happy, they couldn't help but elevate everyone's mood.

Laughing, I answered, "See you shortly."

Stopping at the Palm Park Coffee Shop, I got us both large coffees to go. The girls were friendly and seemed to be glad to see me.

"Oh, Harper, this guy came in a few minutes ago and asked if you came in here on a regular basis. I told him yes. He asked for me to give this to you the next time I saw you." She handed me an envelope.

I turned it over in my hands a couple of times. This was odd. It was just a plain number ten envelope with no writing on the outside.

Since I had a few minutes for the coffees to be ready, I opened the envelope. Pulling out a white sheet of paper. I debated about unfolding it and reading the contents.

Taking a deep breath, I hoped it was not a nasty note that was going to create an undue amount of stress on my already frazzled nerves. It said, "Meet me tonight at eight at the old house."

CHAPTER 6

Life was getting curiosier and curiosier to quote Lewis Carroll. I'd have to tell Ronnie about this. Maybe he'd go with me. I was assuming the old house was where I grew up. Even though I had moved back to Palm Park several months ago, I just never got around to going back and looking at the house I grew up in.

My living in an apartment reflected new decisions, a new way of experiencing life in new forms. The house had been sold years ago, and whatever the owners had chosen to do with the house...well, it was theirs. I didn't care. As far as I was concerned, it was comparable to owning an old coat I had given away to Goodwill. Good memories but no longer relevant to my current life.

Strolling into the pet store was equivalent to walking into a happy ray of sunshine. Ronnie was always happy. His smile could light up the entire state of Florida.

"Honey, honey, honey! Oh, I do love you for bringing me a butter pecan coffee." He promptly snatched it out of my hand. "I did get the right one, right?"

Nodding, I laughed. "Yes, I got us both a butter pecan today."

Placing the coffee on the counter, Ronnie reached into the puppy playpen and pulled out a very enthusiastic little Maltese.

I reached for her. I love puppies and I especially love Maltese dogs. I snuggled with her and let her lick all over my face and neck.

Ronnie grinned. "You still cannot have one of my dogs. We both know you'd forget about taking care of one of my babies."

Much as I hated to admit it, he was right. I'd forget to take the puppy out, I'd forget to feed it, and I'd probably forget its name within a matter of hours, particularly if I was writing a new book. BUT, I could love on any of his dogs as much as I liked.

"So, honey, what is that you need my advice on?"

I explained everything that had happened and ended with, "So, will you go with me to the old house tonight?"

Ronnie slightly frowned. "Harper, unless my memory suddenly has Swiss cheese holes in it, I think your house was torn down about a year ago. Someone was building a larger home on that lot, and I don't know if it was ever finished."

Looking up over his cup, "I'm assuming this means you never went back and looked at it."

I wiggled my eyebrows at him. "No point. I sold it and moved on."

He had a pensive look on his face. "You know, this could be dangerous. Maybe you should call Detective Sam and..."

"It's his day off," I interrupted him.

Ronnie tapped his first finger against his chin, thinking. "Harper, this whole area was chill until you moved back. Girl, what kind of nastiness did you bring back with you from Jacksonville? Please tell me you weren't involved in some weird voodoo stuff."

He looked at me and questioningly and then we both laughed. I wondered the same thing about the bizarre things that kept happening around me since I had moved back to Palm Park. Was this like a weird flu bug or some cosmic demonic fairy dust that somehow managed to find its way onto a poor, unsuspecting writer?

What were the odds of being around two murders in less than six months? It was bad enough when Sarah and I had gone for coffee, only for her to be tragically murdered by a mentally unstable business owner consumed by jealousy. She was now permanently ensconced at a long-term stay-cation resort courtesy of the state of Florida.

Now, I had this new murder that was suddenly in my sphere of existence. Was this the universe giving me a sign I should be writing murder mysteries or was it merely telling me I should stay indoors, write, and never let sunlight hit my pasty white skin? Does thinking these kinds of thoughts make me a double-minded person bouncing around on the ocean of life?

Ronnie was speaking. I could see his lips move but I was thinking. I don't think I multi-task well. So, I said the most intelligent thing I could think of at the moment, "Do what? I know you said something but I, um, was thinking..."

He grinned, "I said that you were living too much in your head, Harper. I also said meeting someone at night was probably not a wise thing to do. You definitely need backup."

Defending my going out at night, I snorted, "It's summertime, Ronnie. It's not going to get dark until about eight-thirty or so. As long as we can see what's going on, everything should be fine."

I wanted him to come with me. Thinking having a man accompany me would ward off any potential issues with meeting the stranger, I attempted to bribe him, I offered, "I'll buy your dinner at Hubba Bubba's."

Rolling his eyes, this was confirmation he was going to go with me, he beamed, "You certainly know the way to my heart. I love Hubba Bubba's. They have the best hushpuppies and fried catfish any-where."

He sighed, "Okay, I'll do it. But we have to come back here before we go over to your old house. My babies need to be able to go out and do their job before bed."

I agreed. "I'll be back around six and we can go then."

Deciding to go by the old place after leav-ing Ronnie, I wanted to check the area ahead of time. I had offered to take one of the little, fluffy white Maltese puppies for a ride, but he was adamant that I wasn't a good choice for that. I was a little irritated about that but, in all honesty, I knew he as right. If, God forbid, I had an accident and something happened to the puppy, I would disappear and never been heard from again.

I thought about the house I grew up in and I had exactly zero feelings about it. Nothing. Not the slightest twinge, no emotional angst, no nothing. It was just something I was going to go look at.

Driving up the brick-lined street, I could see where the house had been torn down. It did appear to be under construction for a new home. The yard contained concrete blocks, wheelbarrows, and similar construction materials, but it appeared that work had been ceased for several months. I could see where weeds had grown up around the building material. Maybe the crew had been called to another job suddenly, but it was odd that no one had come back for their equipment and building material.

Since no one was around. I parked on the street and wandered around the area. There weren't any neighbors close by. The lots in this area had been huge, probably half a football field length or more between houses. I don't remember being overly friendly with neighbors as a kid. Chances of me knowing anyone now were between slim and none and Slim had gone to the Bahamas.

Carefully walking around, I didn't see anything that was screaming, "Danger, Will Robinson, danger!" There had been some concrete walls erected but no roof and the walls only extended about chest height. Maybe the new owners had run out of money, or the bank had taken over the property. Who knows? And I certainly didn't care.

Everything seemed relatively safe to me when Ronnie and I would come back tonight.

The thought did occur to me that I might need to bring a weapon of mass destruction back with me, but I didn't own one and I was fairly sure Ronnie didn't either. I certainly didn't think anything harmful would happen to either me or Ronnie.

I should have paid attention to that thought.

CHAPTER 7

Ronnie and I had a great meal at Hubba Bubba's Fish Camp. It was really just a rustic restaurant sitting over the St. Johns River. You didn't have to worry about accidental tourists finding this place. If they weren't native to Palm Park, the only way they would have found it was only because a local had brought them here. Hubba Bubba's didn't advertise. They weren't on social media. There weren't any signs posted on how to find them. It's just rural Florida at its best.

Ronnie was a little magpie, happy in his environment. The man knew everyone in town. Tons of people came over and spoke with him.

"Why haven't you run for office, Ronnie?" I was chowing down on the all-you-can-eat fried catfish special and I was up to number six. The catfish were as long as my wrist to the tip end of my middle finger. Some folks refer to them as fingerling catfish.

He giggled as he picked up another small fried catfish. "Honey, I don't want to be mayor. I want people to like me. I don't like politics. I just want to own my little pet store and have people know they aren't buying some puppy mill babies. These are little ones chosen by me, bred by responsible owners.

"Also, if I were mayor, I'd have to be in an office and that thought just makes me want to throw up. Nope, my furbabies might bark at me but they don't say ugly things and I don't have to worry about them hurting me."

I reached across the table and placed my hand on top of Ronnie's. He had been the victim of an unprovoked attack several months ago, spent time in ICU, and was fortunate to be back at the pet store.

Telling him what I found at my old place, I ended with, "Who and what do you think is going on?"

He laughed, "Are you sure you're not being pranked on some writer's tv show?"

I rolled my eyes.

"I don't know. Maybe you've gotten involved in a spy operation."

Choking on my iced tea, I managed to get out, "That makes absolutely no sense. I don't know anything that a corporation or the government would want to know about."

He arched his eyebrows. I must say he does it a lot better than I do. "Haven't you heard the old saying, 'I love my country, it's the government I fear'?"

I still didn't know anything. My brain was running at the speed of slow on trying to find a connection to any of these strange happenings. My ex-husband wasn't tied to anything to do with the government. I had no clue about Mason or what he was involved in since I had only just become aware of his existence.

Dear old dad, as far as I could tell, was a musician who just roamed the country visiting bars. Most musicians I know, and I only know two, were simply not the brightest bulbs in the box and I sincerely doubted the CIA, FBI, or any other scrambled letters of a governmental agency would want anything to do with them. They also smoked a lot of an illegal substance that most people in this country would like to see legalized.

It was still very light out when we arrived at the house. In the Florida summertime, daylight started at six a.m. and the bright sun could easily still be shining on everyone until about nine p.m.

There was a blue pickup truck parked in front of the property. No license plate. That should have been a clue that this might not have been one of my brighter ideas to do. I did, however, have the sense to take a picture of the truck with my phone.

I pulled up close to the truck but far enough back that I could escape quickly if I needed to.

We got out and Ronnie looked through the passenger window and announced, "Nothing here, nothing on the seat. It's clean."

We turned to go up the driveway when a man started walking toward us. I hadn't noticed him until just then. It was like he just suddenly appeared. He was wearing jeans, boots, and a tee shirt that said, "Only the good die young."

I smiled and quipped, "Billy Joel." I knew that song.

The man didn't say anything. He didn't look at the front of his shirt. I would have done that since I never remember what I put on in the morning.

Ronnie was being exceptionally quiet, which meant that he was trying to figure out if he knew this man.

The man beckoned us with his forefinger, turned, and started walking back to the far concrete wall. The wall was just tall enough to hide someone if they were crouching. I certainly hoped this wasn't the case.

We had walked forward and stopped just short of the back wall when Ronnie halted. He said loudly, "We're not going any further until you tell us what's going on."

The man either didn't hear Ronnie or he had decided to ignore us. He disappeared around a small shed in the back. I hadn't really noticed it before. The shade from the huge oak tree had hidden it. At least that's what I was telling myself because I hated to admit I wasn't being all that observant; I was more focused on the man. Who am I kidding? I wanted to be alert in case someone jumped out from behind the half-wall of the house.

"Ronnie, that shed wasn't here when I was a kid."

He shrugged. He was probably right, what difference did it make, especially since I had no intention of going that far.

"Unt uh, I'm not going somewhere that far from the street." I finally grew a spine.

Too many weird things had happened, and I wasn't willing to participate in anything that might cause me bodily harm. I also noticed Ronnie had graciously allowed me to lead. He's a wimp but, then again, I already knew that. I am too which is the reason why I can spot it in others so quickly.

Half-turning, "If you want to go ahead, I'm fine with that but I'm not going any further."

He grinned and bobbed his head. "Yoo hoo! Yoo hoo! Sir, sir, you need to come back out here."

Crickets. If whoever it was thought we were brave enough to wander back there on our own, they were sadly mistaken. We both had a yellow streak down our backs the size of the Ganges

River. I was okay with being called a chicken. I'd stand up and own it.

The hair on my neck was a little damp. Maybe it was just sweat instead of my silly nerves...that's what I was trying to convince myself. I was trying to coax my nerves into believing that they were an early warning system for possible mayhem in my life but, much as I hate to say it, other than being a little sweaty, I wasn't getting much direction in the way of being in danger. Apparently, I have a lousy personal GPS system.

"Harper, honey, nothing's happening. Let's just go back to the car."

That's when I heard the cha-chunk of a shotgun pump. That's never a sign of welcoming hospitality. I turned and took off running down the driveway. Ronnie sprinted past me like a scared bunny in front of a bunch of hungry greyhounds.

He slid into the passenger side just as I dive-bombed into the driver's seat. My hands were shaking so badly that I was having a hard time even punching the start button on my car. Finally, it started, and we peeled off.

We both heard the shotgun explosion as stumbled into the car. What was even scarier was the dirt that bounced up and splattered against the car door. I was beyond grateful that neither one of us was digging little steel pellets out of our bodies. Buckshot could make anyone turn into instant hamburger helper.

Ronnie was hyperventilating, gulping in deep breaths of air before he managed to speak. "Harper, I don't like playing with you. This is dangerous. I'm not doing it again."

My neurological synapses were not firing on all cylinders. I was shaking. I was also not sure when the last time I had taken a deep breath. We were back on the main road, and I pulled into the McDonald's parking lot.

"Ronnie..."

"Nope, not doing it again," he gasped out. He was pale and shaking. I hoped I wasn't going to have to take him to the emergency room.

"Not what I was going to say," I semi-hissed out. I was lying. "I was going to say why do you think that guy used a shotgun on us?"

He shook his head. "Don't know, don't care. Not my circus, not my monkey. Take me home."

"Ronnie..."

He turned to me, tears in his eyes, "Harper, please take me home. My nerves can't take this. I'm already on medication from when that last guy tried to kill me."

His voice was steadily increasing until he wailed, "My babies need me. I can't let anything happen to my babies."

While I'm not normally an overly compassionate individual, I did experience sympathy for him. He had been traumatized several months ago when a man had beaten him up so badly that he ended up in ICU in the hospital. He was just getting back to being his old self.

"Ronnie, do you mind if we swing by my place real quick?" I paused for a moment, "I want to make sure no one broke in."

He could only nod while he was dabbing at his eyes with his blue and white silk handkerchief.

I started a nervous laugh and pointed at his handkerchief. "Ronnie, those colors look like they belong in the Kentucky Derby."

He was huffy. "These colors are very fashionable. I saw them when I was in Atlanta last week. But I'm glad you like them."

That's Ronnie, take a negative and turn it into a positive.

We both went into my apartment, checked all the windows, and, yes, of course, I checked the shower and closet. I had seen the shower scene in the movie Psycho, and it had scared the holy bejabbers out of me. I'm not sure what I would have done if someone was hiding behind the shower curtain.

I was standing in my bedroom thinking. I could hear Ronnie opening my refrigerator door.

"Harper, honey, I'm taking your bottle of Pinot Grigio home with me."

My eyebrows decided to meet in the middle. "What did you say, Ronnie?" Maybe I hadn't heard him right.

"I said I'm taking your bottle of Pinot home with me."

"Don't!" I shouted as I ran through the living room and into the kitchen.

He looked befuddled and held out the bottle to me. "I, I, I just thought it'd be okay," he stuttered.

"No, it's not that, Ronnie. You're certainly welcome to whatever's in the house but that's not mine. I don't drink white wine." I was trying to explain but everything came out in a rush.

Grabbing the bottle from him, I pointed at the top of the bottle. "Someone has opened it and left it here. That can't be good in any sense of the word."

Ronnie whipped out his phone. "Enough of playing games, Harper! It's time for the cops. There is just too much craziness going on. I'm calling Detective

Sam." He was nervously tapping his fingers on the countertop.

I guess Sam wasn't answering his phone because Ronnie left a message. He texted a message to someone. "Please take me home, Harper, I've had all the excitement I can stand for one day."

Nodding, I couldn't blame him. My nerves were shot as well. My thoughts were bouncing around like ping pong balls during the Chinese Olympics. Nothing was making sense.

I didn't think anyone was actually trying to kill me. Scare me, yes; but killing me, no. But what were they trying to scare me off from? I didn't know anything...or, at least, I didn't think I did.

Arriving at Ronnie's cottage, I saw his friend Donnie's car. I did a side-eye glance at him.

"I need someone to come spend the night with me. Donnie was free for the evening. He's not going to let anyone get past the front door."

Grinning, "I need some of your friends, Ronnie. I want someone to protect me."

He harrumphed, "You need to make nice nice with Detective Sam and you won't have that problem."

All I could do was nod my head. I didn't want to have to explain why I didn't want a romantic relationship right now, although the thought had occurred to me on several occasions.

Donnie came out to the car. He had on blue camos. I didn't even know cammies came in any other color than green and brown. But, then again, I'm not a fashionista.

Leaving the two of them, I headed back to my apartment. Pulling into my parking spot at the complex later, I noticed Sam's unmarked police car several spaces down.

He was waiting for me by my apartment door. "I understand you need some help."

CHAPTER 8

It was all I could do to keep from having a silly schoolgirl grin on my face. What was it about this guy who kept getting in my head? Maybe I did want a romantic relationship with him that I was suppressing. He was cute, had a dimple in his cheek, dark wavy hair although it was short, and usually a very nice personality. I think I might test it on occasion.

Managing to suppress my ever-widening grin, I tampered down my emotional, wayward thoughts and merely answered, "Yep. Ronnie called you?"

"Yep."

Oh, great, now we're playing one-word games. I couldn't blame him since I was the one who had started it.

Plunging ahead, I wanted him to know everything that had occurred. "Sam, did he tell you everything that has happened? By the way, would you like some hot tea?"

"Harper, I'm not sure what's going on here." He scratched the back of his head and nodded his head for the tea. I turned on the electric tea kettle to heat up the water. Yes, I could put the cups in the microwave and heat the water that way except I'm somewhat of a purist when it comes to my tea. I wanted water heated in an electric tea kettle. It just seems so homey, so British, so author-ish...it just makes me feel good.

Coffee, I just drink whatever is put in front of me. Putting a teaspoon of the Blood Orange loose tea I had recent-ly purchased from Queen Bee June at Steapers in the tea ball, I turned and started to reach for a cup for each of us and realized Sam had already pulled two down from the cabinet.

He smiled and turned his palm over when I blinked in surprise at him. I was actually a little dumbfounded at his "Try-ing to be helpful."

I didn't know what to say. In the few years that I had been married, never once had my ex ever handed me any type of utensil - plate, glass, or cup. I guess he thought those things just magically appeared on the countertop or table for his dining enjoyment. He also never put anything in the sink or dishwasher regardless of how many times I asked him. I think we had separate lives long before we divorced. I don't what possessed either one of us to get married. We were misfits from the get-go.

I think my brain slid into some type of vortex, more like the spin cycle of a washing machine, but I didn't have the social coping skills on how to handle this nicety from Sam. This was something I never had happen before. I tried to think how Oprah would have responded to this back in her tv heyday. I couldn't recall if she had ever done a show on the social skills needed to survive for this type of situation.

Martha Stewart, now she's a demi-goddess of all things pertaining to the home, I had watched Martha a lot longer and much more often than I ever had Oprah.

What would Queen Martha do? Taking a deep breath, I breathed out a soft, "Thank you."

The tea kettle let its steam-generated long sigh out indicating that the water was ready to be poured into the cups.

How long had I been standing there contemplating the appropriate response to Sam? It seemed like hours but was probably only a couple of seconds when I said, "Thank you."

I felt like I was living in an alternative universe when he was around. There was real and then there was whatever was whirling around in my brain. Was

I going crazy? Early dementia? Maybe I have undiagnosed Asperger's. I'd like to say it might have been all the weed I had smoked back in college except that would be a lie. The two times I had tried it, and I really did make a great effort to inhale the yellow smoke deep into my lungs because I so desperately wanted to be cool and fit in with my college roommates, it had made me incredibly drowsy to the point that I basically went to sleep right where I was. I had tumbled over on the couch, my eyes were shut, and I was snoozing away in la-la land almost immediately. I had been told I wasn't a fun, party person. So much for me being voted Miss Life-of-the-Party.

Sam raised his eyebrows. Okay, he must have asked a question. It probably had to do with him wanting to know if I had any sugar since we were drinking tea.

"The sugar and honey are in that cabinet." I pointed to the one next to the cups.

"Good guess but that wasn't what I asked," he grinned. That cute dimple in his cheek got me every time. Were these merely some type of emotions that I had kept repressed all these years? Perhaps it was some type of weird professional writer overload that I had never heard about.

"What I asked was if the man at your old house was your dad?"

I shook my head, hopefully, scattering my errant thoughts to the wind...although there was no wind blowing through my apartment, not even the air conditioning was on. "Even though I haven't seen him in years, there was absolutely nothing about him that would indicate he was."

I was befuddled, swiping my hand through my hair. "Sam, the guy never said anything. That's what was weird."

He blew on his hot tea before responding. A twinkle in his eye, "So, the fact that he pumped a shotgun at you wasn't strange? Is there something in your background you want to share with me?" He was almost laughing.

I flushed with pink creeping across my cheeks and grinned. "Yeah, well, I see your point. I was just going over everything in detail. Honestly, I kind of wanted it to be my dad, happy that it wasn't, and I'm more confused than ever about this whole thing. There is, literally, nothing that's making any sense."

He leaned toward me, his eyebrows furrowing. "I agree, Harper, but this is not random. The guy had the opportunity to kill both you and Ronnie. He had no way of knowing you were bringing anyone with you. If he kills one of you, he might as well kill both of you since, if he were ever caught, he'd be doing life anyway. This is more like a warning but the question what are you being warned about?"

I chewed the inside of my cheek. My hands were wrapped around the cup, the warmth felt good. It also helped to keep them still, not shaking. I didn't want to admit how much all of this was upsetting me.

"Here's something else for you to think about. The guy knew how to handle a shotgun. It wasn't like he accidentally let loose buckshot into your car door. He deliberately sprayed it into the dirt near your car. He meant to scare you." He was analyzing the details of what I had told him. I could tell he was concerned, his eyebrows were drawn together, his lips in a firm straight line, and his facial muscles were tight.

Chewing on my lower lip, I slowly dipped my head down in agreement. "You're right. I hadn't actually thought of it in that way."

"I be a detective."

We both laughed. The laughter felt good. Maybe I should try doing it more often. I'd have to ask Ronnie about all these errant thoughts that had either escaped from the nut house or were from outer space aliens trying to pollute the empty air inside my skull. Ronnie was better than a paid psychiatrist, he was also cheaper. Buying a meal here and there was well worth it to me.

Also, he was a cheap date. It's not like we were going to some high-end Brazilian steak house for one meal and where I'd have to be eating beanie-weenies for the rest of the month.

My tea was still very warm. "Well, 'Mr. I be a detective' what do you think is going on here?"

Sam looked at me over the top of his cup. "I don't think it's you this person is after. I think you're being used as bait."

Staring at him blankly for a moment, I finally uttered the only coherent thing I could think of. "Me? For what? I don't know anything."

"I don't think it's about what you do or do not know. I think someone thinks you're either in touch with your dad or you know how to get in touch with him. They, in essence, want you to lead them to him."

Snorting, I rolled my eyes. "Seriously, if that were the case, they know diddly squat about my relationship with my dad.

"In fact," I was gathering steam on this new thought, "there's virtually nothing on the internet that even remotely connects me with dear old dad."

Sam shrugged. "Who knows? Maybe Mickey said something to the wrong person or, more likely, he's up to his eyeballs in something and mentioned your name to keep him out of trouble."

I started to laugh. "Really?"

Sam took a big gulp of his tea. "You do know..."

"Come on, Sam, I've told you umpteen times, I know so little about the man that it's ridiculous."

He ignored me and continued, "he has an extensive arrest record across the country."

CHAPTER 9

That wasn't the best news I'd ever heard. However, I couldn't compute how that even applied to me. So what if he had umpteen arrest records? The man was a musician and travelled a lot...or, at least, I had surmised that he did. I had a now-deceased half-brother that I knew nothing about. I was taking a wild guess that dear old dad had probably populated a number of, um, fields from one coast to the other. Not my problem.

"So what? How does that affect me? I've only lived three places in my entire life...Palm Park, Gainesville at the University of Florida, go Gators, and in Jacksonville."

I was mildly curious. "Do I dare ask what he was arrested for? Wait!" I held up my hand. "Let me guess, drunk and disorderly conduct, public drunkenness, urinating in public."

The dimple showed up again. I felt squishy inside, not naughty squishy, but happy squishy. What was wrong with me?

"Mostly. But here's the crazy thing, his file shows up as classified on the FBI's website."

Shut the front door! What in the heck?! Wait. What does that even mean? My brain was shooting off bottle rockets of wayward thoughts, none of them exploding too brightly. They must be duds.

"Let me guess, way back in the day he belonged to some anti-Vietnam hippie group or something."

Sam shrugged. "Without me jumping through a lot of hoops, I don't know."

This was a lot like playing a puzzle without a picture of how the completed puzzle should look.

"What about Mason? What's his background?"

"Nothing much. Surfer dude, worked odd jobs here and there. Didn't have so much as a speeding ticket."

I guess I must watch too many spy movies because my thought was that Mason was collateral damage.

"He was used as a warning to Mickey."

Cocking my head at Sam, "What does that mean?"

My phone went off and showed an unknown number ID. Looking at Sam, "Hello."

"You left too soon last night."

It takes a lot to make me mad but whoever this was had just pushed the wrong button on this side of civility. "What do you mean? You tried to kill me last night!" I screeched.

A slight chuckle. "It was a warning. You've been warned." The call was disconnected.

I had already punched speaker on my phone so that Sam heard everything.

Looking at him with wide eyes. "Are there two different things going on here?"

The living room glass shattered. Sam grabbed the top of my shoulders and pushed me to the floor. I dropped my cup where it broke into nine million pieces. That was my favorite cup. Why do I wonder about weird stuff like that when someone just fired a shot through my window? Focus, Harper, focus.

For whatever reason, Sam tossed his cup across the now broken glass window area. I was going to have to buy another mug because that one died by death by high-powered rifle.

"Give me another cup."

Carefully opening the dishwasher, I handed him a dirty cup. If it was going to be shot, killed, and destroyed, it didn't make any difference if it was clean or dirty.

He tossed it in front of the window again. It fell to the floor. It broke instead of being shot.

Standing up, Sam said, "Whoever this is, they're a pro. To hit a coffee mug through a window requires some skill and precision."

"Military?" I questioned as I stood up.

"More than likely. You don't get that good without a lot of practice and ammo."

My phone rang again. I answered it warily. "Yes?"

"Toss up another cup. I need another practice shot." I immediately dropped to the floor on my knees and handed the phone to Sam. I'm a coward, what can I say?

His voice was icy cold as he punched the speaker button. "What do you want?"

The voice laughed. "World peace, Sam, world peace. I wondered how long it would take for you to get on Harper's phone."

Sam's brow furrowed. "Who is this?"

"Not your best friend. Good luck, buddy."

He stared at the phone for a few minutes after the caller disconnected before saying, "I've heard that voice before, but it's been a long time."

I gasped, "So, you know this guy?"

"Know probably isn't the best word to use, but, yeah, I think so. I've heard this voice before, I just don't know from where."

"Maybe you're the connection?" I tentatively offered.

He snorted as he walked over to the now breezy non-existent glass window. "If that were the case, I would have been dead by now."

Turning his back to the window, I actually cringed because if the shooter were still there, Sam was an easy not-to-be-missed target. He eyed the living room wall. I noticed a hole about the size of my thumb. "Um..."

He was looking down at the floor, picking up a casing, he examined it for a moment, turning it over and over in his hand. "Military grade."

I just nodded. I thought we had already established that fact. I guess it was a guy thing to announce that. It was just a smushed-up mushroom-looking piece of metal as far as I was concerned.

"Harper, he's just trying to scare you."

Snorting, "He's doing a fine job of it. If he thinks I'm going to lead him to dear old dad, I still don't know any more than I did before...which is nothing."

My phone pinged indicating a new message. I showed it to Sam who immediately put his finger to his lips as he searched under the coffee table, looked up at the ceiling light fixture, and pointed. There was a small square box at the top of the ceiling fan.

The phone pinged again. I swiped the message. "Where's the money?"

Pointing at the text, I said loudly, "Who-ever you are, I haven't seen Mickey in years, and I have absolutely no clue what you mean about where's the money. If you think I can lead you to him, you're just a special kind of stupid." I drew out the word stupid so it sounded like stoopid.

The next text was just a finger pointing at me emoji. If Sam hadn't been there, I would have been a willy-nilly basket-case. My nerves weren't in the best of shape now but were vastly superior to what they would have been if I were home alone.

Sam stood up on my coffee table and pulled the small square box from the ceiling fixture. Grinning, he tossed it on the floor and brought his heel down crushing it. To make doubly sure it would not transmit sound ever again, he chucked it in the sink and turned on the water. Electronics and water are not a match made in heaven.

I was sweating buckets. This was way past lady-like perspiration. I asked, "Did you just sign my death warrant by doing that?"

He lifted his shoulders and then let them drop. "Doubtful. He could have killed you many times before now. He, or whomever he's working for, think you know something about Mickey."

Protesting as I started to pick up the large pieces of glass on the floor, "I don't know anything."

I hate housecleaning in general. The thought of cleaning up this mess was nauseating. There was nothing mentally or physically in me that wanted to scoop, sweep, or mop up the thousand and one little shards of glass now decorating my floor.

There was a knock at my door. I started to hyperventilate, my heart pounded and then tried to convince myself that if the sniper was going to kill me, he wouldn't do it by knocking on the door.

Sam looked through the peephole and then flung the door open as he stepped away from it. There was a box sitting on the welcome mat. I just looked at it, unsure what to do. I hadn't ordered anything online.

He picked it up and placed it on the kitchen countertop slowly turning it. "Got a label on it with your name and address."

Sam whipped out a knife from somewhere in his cargo pants and cut open the box. I peered over his shoulder. I gasped. Assuming that what I was looking at in the large, clear, plastic bag was not cane sugar or a vast quantity of baking soda, this was a gift that carried a felony charge of years to be spent in a government less-than-desirable resort if I was convicted. I don't look good in orange.

The fact that there was a law enforcement officer next to me looking at the same white, powdery substance didn't really make me feel any better since the box was addressed to me. I didn't know if Sam thought I was trafficking illicit drugs or not.

Let's face it, drug dealers make a lot more money than writers do. But, then again, why would I be living in an apartment if I were selling drugs? Hopefully, that thought had already occurred to Sam.

"Want to sell it and move out of the country?"

I hoped he was kidding when he said that although he had a poker face plastered on. My throat had seized up and I was trying to say something, but nothing was coming out. I shook my head. I could feel sweat running down my back. I vaguely wondered how much water weight I had lost in the past several hours. It had to be at least twenty pounds...hopefully.

There was absolutely no way I was going to jail...for any reason. I was trying to think of a way to escape. What countries don't have an extradition agreement with the U.S.? Given time, I could figure out what I needed to do but, standing next to a detective who had the power to take away my freedom, my brain went into meltdown mode. Three Mile Island or Chernobyl meltdown, where nothing no longer existed, were small compared to what was running rampant through my mind.

"Uh..."

Sam patted my hand, grinning. "You look like you've seen a ghost. I'm joking. There's no way I would even try to sell that much coke on the street."

Pausing with a slight smile and his eyes scanning my face, "You're fine, Harper. I'm not going to arrest you. I know you didn't have anything to do with this."

My phone rang causing both of us to jump. I punched speaker and cautiously answered. "Hello."

The voice was merry. "Well, hello, daughter of mine."

CHAPTER 10

I almost fainted. I felt like I was in the wind tunnel of a tornado. I was Dorothy in the Wizard of Oz, and I hadn't been smacked in the head. Taking a deep breath, I noticed Sam had placed his hand in the middle of my back. I was assuming it was because if I did faint, it would make it easier for him to guide me down to the floor.

"Mickey?" I managed to eke out, I couldn't bring myself to call him Dad. Why would I, given that I haven't seen or talked to the man in twenty-something years?

He sighed, almost giggling, "Well, I guess it is a little bit too much to expect you to call me Dad. Anyway, I sent you a box. I'm assuming that you received it."

Nodding my head and then realizing he couldn't see me. "Yes. Why are you sending hundreds of thousands of dollars of what appears to be cocaine to me? I don't do drugs and I certainly don't sell them."

"Which makes you the perfect recipient to receive my package. Please note, this is not a gift. That is my property."

Sam stopped himself from snapping his fingers and doing a high five with me. He had a big grin on his face. I wondered if he'd get a promotion after busting dear old dad on this.

He rolled his two fingers in a circular motion to keep me talking with Mickey.

"Yeah, so what am I supposed to do with this?" I snapped. "Does this have anything to do with Mason getting murdered?"

"That was very unfortunate, and it wasn't supposed to happen but certain, ah, people weren't willing to wait on some, um, items." Mickey sounded breezy. Mason's death didn't seem to faze him in the slightest. Either the man had a very cold heart, which did not bode well for me if anything nefarious came up...like a choice of whether I should live or die... or the man could hide his emotions very well. I was betting he had a cold heart.

Exploding, I slammed my hand down on the counter, "Listen, your son was murdered, and you don't have the slightest reaction to it? All you're interested in is the coke? What kind of mo..."

Sam was waving his hands at me and silently mouthing, "Don't."

Mickey's voice dropped and slowed down, "You know nothing about what's going on. Just for the record, Mason was not my biological son."

"Irrelevant!" I almost screamed at him. "He was still related to you! How can you be so heartless? Oh, yes, it's easy because you've done it before."

This time his voice was flat. "Bring the box over to the Cantina near the Naval Air Station. Ask for Fat Freddy and give it to him only. No one else. Fat Freddy looks just like you would imagine him to look."

"NO!" I shouted. Sam was waving at me, his eyes wide. I ignored him. "NO! If I get caught with this, I'll go to jail and I'm not going to jail for any reason. And I'm especially not going to jail for you."

Mickey's voice was taunting, "I see you haven't lost any of your exuberance from childhood."

I disconnected the call and threw my phone across the room. I was breathing heavily. Tears had sprung to my eyes, more from anger than anything else.

"Harper, we have to get this guy." Sam's voice was urgent. "Call him back and agree to do it."

"NO!" I wailed. "What if someone screws up and I'm arrested on felony drug charges? I can't spend even one night in jail. No, no, no! This is my life we're talking about. Whoever these people are, they're willing to kill."

Breaking down into embarrassing deep, gut-wrenching sobs, I huffed out, "I don't want to die."

Surprising me, Sam wrapped his arms around me. It felt good. "Listen, I'm not going to let anything happen to you. This is a big-time drug deal. It means there's not just one or two people involved in this. Chances are there may be some Navy personnel involved as well."

I looked up at him, wiping the tears from my face. "Why?"

"You live in Palm Park. He's asking you to meet him near NAS at a club he's probably supposed to play at."

Interrupting him, "No. He said for me to give it to Fat Freddy. He didn't say the first thing about meeting him there."

"He's still probably playing there and whatever is going on will take the spotlight off him."

"Bait, I'm the bait dog," I grumbled as I looked at the kitchen countertop to see if I had a tissue box there.

The phone rang. It took several rings before I found where I had thrown it across the room.

"Yeah." I didn't see any point in being polite anymore.

Mickey picked up right where we had left off in the conversation. "Give the box to Fat Freddy and leave. That's it. Do it tonight somewhere between nine and ten. There's no reason for you to come and watch me play with my band."

I snorted. He ignored me and continued. "Fat Freddy will ask you who your favorite author is. Give him your name because," he paused almost laughing, "I'm assuming you are your own favorite author."

Rolling my eyes at Sam, I gave a three-finger salute to Mickey although he couldn't see it.

"Yeah, okay." I was reluctant.

"Harper, this is a warning. If you bring law enforcement, the FBI, or anyone else with you and Fat Freddy is arrested, you won't live to have your morning coffee." He hung up.

I was shaking so badly you could turn me into a walking massage machine.

"I'm going to die, I'm going to die, I'm going to die," I kept repeating over and over, totally unaware that Sam had placed both hands on each arm and was gently shaking me.

His voice was gentle. "Harper, you're going to be fine. We're not going to do anything that will jeopardize your life. Trust me on this."

My teeth were chattering. Fear does strange things to a human body. I was overwhelmed with sensory overload with my brain, my body, and my teeth. I wanted to hide. I didn't want to adult anymore.

I discovered I was sitting on the couch while Sam was making phone calls. I guess he must have placed me there. I was in the vortex of life seemingly, maddingly, spinning out of control.

"Okay, here's what's going to happen." As Sam explained the evening's plan, my brain slowly started to function. I only knew this because I felt a slight electrical surge indicating a new thought pattern. It was seeking to find what was wrong with the plan. Nothing, not one thing. Did I dare to hope that maybe, just maybe, I would be safe, and nothing would happen to me, and that maybe I could be eating pancakes or waffles in the morning?

"Oh, by the way," Sam interrupted my train of thought, "I'm having your window boarded up in a few minutes."

That was thoughtful of him. I was thinking I was going to be spending the night in a hotel where I could have a free breakfast buffet first thing in the morning. I could still do that. I know I would feel a lot safer.

That's my plan and I'm sticking to it.

"I know we have some clear packing tape at the office and..."

I sniffed, "The only loophole I see in the entire plan is getting that box into my car without me being killed."

"Not to worry. We're going to put the couch throw over it along with some of your clothes on top and put it in your car.

It will look like you're moving out for the night."

"About that. I am. I'm going to spend the night at the hotel."

I expected an argument but didn't get it. Much as I hate to admit it, I was almost disappointed that I didn't receive any pushback about that.

"My cleaning lady is going to come over tomorrow morning and clean up this mess. Spending the night in the hotel is probably a good idea."

The only thing I've got to say is his mama trained him right. It was kind of strange that a detective had a cleaning lady but maybe...I could speculate on that topic for hours and still never come up with the right answer.

He was a gentleman; he did carry the box and my clothes out to my car. I followed him to the police station and parked in the garage.

Even though Palm Park is a small town, they did have a parking garage. Sam had already made arrangements for me to take an unmarked police car to meet Fat Freddy. Fortunately, this was an impounded vehicle that didn't have 'cop car' screaming all over it.

I drove the hour up to NAS, and found the club, it kind of resembled a strip club. It was in a dingy, tired strip shopping center, and walked in. It was dark. There was a band playing at the far end of the room. I made zero attempt to see if Mickey was playing. Scanning the bar area, I saw a very large man wearing a hideous Florida shirt with pink flamingos and green palm trees. He had an unlit cigar stuffed in the corner of his mouth. I walked over to him. He looked me up and down in a way that made me feel like I was naked.

I was nervous. "Um, are you Freddy?"

He didn't answer and continued to leer at me. It was loud in here. I never looked at the stage, I hoped if Mickey were on stage, he'd see that I was following his instructions. Maybe he didn't hear me, so I spoke louder. "Are you Freddy?"

Bobbing his head, he took his unlit cigar out of his mouth. "I'm Fat Freddy. You wanna drink?"

I blinked my eyes slowly trying to process everything while trying to act confident. I was scared. "Um, no, thank you."

"So, what's a classy broad like you doing in a place like this?"

Okay, this was the right guy, but he didn't ask any questions like Mickey said he would do. This still felt like a setup to me. I didn't want to be here any longer than necessary.

"I have something for you." Okay, this probably wasn't the smartest thing to say to a guy who was at least one hundred pounds overweight and apparently thought of himself as a ladies man.

If I thought he had leered at me before, it wasn't anything like he was doing now. There was sheer lust on his face, and he made no effort to conceal it. He was gross.

"Yeah, I'll bet you do, darlin'. Let's say we go in the back. I have a private room." Fat Freddy was almost drooling. Ugh, totally disgusting. I wanted to kill Mickey right now. He wasn't worth going to jail over but the thought was dancing at the fore-front of my mind.

"I mean..." I was struggling to find the words to get the box out of the car and into this guy's hand. I wanted to be rid of this craziness. It's one thing to write about it in a book. It's another to have to live it. I like calmness. This wasn't it.

Finally, I spit it out. "I've got a box I'm supposed to give you. Do you want me to bring it through the front door or do you have a vehicle I can put it in?"

I could see it in his little beady eyes set in a florid face. He was greedy. Not my problem. I was told to give it to him and whatever happened after that wasn't my concern.

"Drive your car around to the back. There's a blue truck back there by the garbage dumpster. Put the box on the passenger's seat. Then you can leave or come back in here and we'll par-tay." He licked his lips.

I wanted to barf. I didn't say anything and turned around to walk out the door when he tapped me on the shoulder.

Turning back around, "What?" I glared at him.

"I don't know if I trust you, honey, but, if this is a setup, you'll wish you'd never been here." The lustful look on his face had turned into a hardened, threatening expression. He scared me. He wasn't just a fat boy with lustful thoughts, this was a guy I was sure had killed someone in his past.

"Trust me, I already wish that." I twisted around his hand and walked out the door.

Driving around the back of the building, I looked to see if I saw any police officers or anyone with guns. Not seeing anyone back there, I did spot the truck and pulled up close to it.

Looking around nervously, there really wasn't anyone back here and only a few vehicles. I opened the truck's passenger side door, left it ajar so I could put the box in there easily. I continued to look around as I picked up the box and then shoved it in the truck. I would not make a good spy, my nerves would do me in.

I also slid a tracker under the car seat before slamming the truck door shut. The sound was a lot noisier than I had anticipated. By this time, I was sure I had lost at least ten pounds in sweat alone just in the past several hours. I was more nervous than a cat on a hot tin roof. Getting back in the car, I borderline peeled out of the parking lot.

Taking deep breaths all the way back to the police station, I was making mental notes that I probably should take up yoga. Anything that would calm my nerves on a regular basis could only be a good thing.

Arriving, Sam greeted me in the garage. "How'd it go?"

I told him everything that had transpired. We had decided I wouldn't wear a wire in case I was searched.

"Nothing happened in the parking lot?"

I shook my head. "I've had all the fun I can stand, Sam. I'm going to the hotel."

An officer came through the station doors, spotted us, and waved at Sam to come inside.

Taking this as my cue to leave, I got in my car and left. Let law enforcement deal with whatever was going on. As far as I was concerned this was no longer my circus and no longer my monkey.

As I was driving to the hotel, I jumped when I realized there were flashing lights behind me. I was in sheer panic mode. What if the cops were going to arrest me now? Quickly looking at the speedometer, I noticed I was actually five miles under the speed limit. Surely, that couldn't be the reason for the flashing lights. I pulled over to the side of the road, four police cars went flying by me with blinking red and blue lights but no sirens.

My stress level was already way over the top. I'd like to say once the cars passed me, my nerves settled down, but I'd be lying. Yes, I vaguely wondered what was happening, but I didn't care enough to give it much more thought.

I wish I had.

CHAPTER 11

Checking into the hotel, all I could think about was taking a long, hot shower and then falling into bed.

That shower felt so good. Stepping out into the room, I discovered a man sitting in the chair, legs crossed, arms folded in his lap, and a shock of brown hair hanging down on his forehead, the rest of his hair was tied back in a ponytail.

I felt weak and grabbed the bathroom door frame.

"Who, who are you? How did you get in here?"

The man simply smiled before answering. "Thanks for delivering the box. Unfortunately, you now know what was in it."

"But, but..." I stuttered. The room was spinning. Was I going to die in a hotel room? Was this Mickey? Then I noticed he was holding a gun in his lap. All the sweat and perspiration I had just washed off in a very relaxing shower, possibly the last one I would ever have, was now back in full force running down my back.

Whatever tiny little bit of adrenaline I had left in my body sparked to life. I was mad.

"Who are you?" I demanded, straightening my posture and readjusting my nightgown. "How did you get in here?"

The man continued to smile and waved his gun at the bed. "Sit down and I'll tell you a story."

I sat down. There was nothing within reach that I could throw at him. A king-size bed pillow wouldn't cause any damage to a man with a gun.

"By the way, nice to actually meet you after twenty years."

Yes, this was dear old dad. Looking closely at him, I did not see any family resemblance whatsoever.

"We don't look anything alike," I stated flatly.

Mickey kind of chuckled. "That's because I'm not your dad."

My eyebrows shot to the moon. "Who are you then?" I demanded. "Aren't you Mickey Rogers?"

Grinning, "Oh, yeah, I'm Mickey Rogers but I'm not your biological dad."

He paused, watching me closely, "Or maybe I am." He shrugged. "Who knows and I don't care."

A gut punch of gigantic proportions hit me. Was my whole life a lie? Had my mother not told the truth about me? Emotions that I didn't know I had welled up within me and I did the most shocking thing I think I have ever done.

I jumped up from the bed and flew the few steps to where he was sitting in the chair. I hit him as hard as I could in the nose. I felt something in my right hand break. I quickly glanced at my hand to make sure all of my digits and knuckles were intact. They were, it was Mickey's nose I broke. Blood squirted out of it.

To say we were both surprised was an understatement. He had let loose the gun in his lap as both hands went to his nose as his head snapped back. Who knew I had such power? I certainly didn't. I had never ever hit someone before. It was weird for me to be this physical with anyone ever. I had the presence of mind to grab the gun and backed up while pointing it at him.

He said a couple of choice words that weren't in the hotel's Gideon Bible. He started to push up from the chair when I snapped, "Don't. Even. Think. About. It."

He laughed and continued to push up from the chair. "You're not going to shoot me."

I felt the gun fire. I swear I don't think I did it. I don't remember squeezing the trigger, although my nerves may have taken over my hands and caused the gun to propel a bullet into Mickey's leg. He screamed. I just looked at the gun, horrified. I am a peace-loving individual or, at least, that's what I've always thought. This was the first time I had ever held a gun in my hands and now I've maimed someone, possibly for life. I was hyperventilating and my hands were shaking uncontrollably. I was afraid to put the gun down because I wasn't sure if Mickey could get to it. My brain was telling me if he could get to it, then he'd probably kill me. He had already indicated that much earlier. I wasn't ready to die.

The hotel phone rang. I carefully eased over to the phone on the nightstand and picked it up. "Hello?"

The voice on the other end said, "Ma'am, are you okay? We've already called the police. Just say 'cat' if you're okay or 'dog' if you need help."

That was a no-brainer. "No, I didn't bring my dog with me."

"Got it. Thank you."

I was trying to take a deep breath, but my lungs were refusing to take in more than a couple of very shallow gulps.

Mickey was moaning, bent over holding his leg around the knee area.

"You witch!" Okay, that wasn't exactly the word he used but it was close enough. It wasn't a word I ever wanted to be called. I went out of my way to be nice to everyone.

"Hey, be careful about using that word," I admonished, still pointing the gun at him, "it's not one I like."

He said it again. Much as I wanted to go over and slap him, I had better sense and knew if I got within arm's reach of him, he could probably overpower me and get the gun. I wasn't going to allow that to happen.

Backing up and easing toward the door, I reached behind me to open it just as

I heard the slight click of the hotel card being inserted into the reader.

A police officer pushed the door open, holding a gun in his right hand and pointing it into the room. I moved over to the side and dropped my hand holding the gun down.

Another officer entered the room, looked at Mickey, and then looked at me. "Ma'am, what's happening here?"

Mickey was trying to tell his side of the story which did not resemble the truth in any way, shape, or form. Both officers were ignoring him. I guess I looked more harmless than he did. I also surmised that a female holding a gun on a man with both a bloody nose and a bleeding leg might indicate to the officers that said female was attempting to defend herself.

I quickly told him what had happened and then said, "Detective Sam Needles knows me and what's happening."

He just nodded and stepped out into the hallway. I assumed it was to call Sam.

A few minutes later, EMTs came into the room and guided Mickey over to the gurney in the hallway while he was doing the one-legged hop walk.

I was still trying to process everything that was going on. The battery in my brain needed to be recharged.

"How did Mickey get into my room? The door was locked." I asked the first officer. He looked over at the other cop and nodded. He left.

The first officer smiled, I had already given him Mickey's gun, "We'll find out. Do you think you're going to be okay? You've had a lot happen."

Really? I was in such a state of overwhelm I wouldn't have been able to define the word normal if my life depended on it. I suspected it was what most people had in their lives...normal. Boring. Quiet. Something I had in my life for years when I lived in Jacksonville. Ever since I moved back to Palm Park, there was more craziness that seemed to surround me on a regular basis. I missed the quiet, the peace, the boring part of life. I was bordering on longing for it to return.

The other officer appeared. "I've just arrested the check-in guy downstairs.

Mickey gave him a hundred dollars for another card to your room. Told the guy he was your dad and wanted to surprise you on your birthday."

I shook my head. "Isn't that illegal? That becomes a major safety issue for single women."

They both nodded.

"By the way, Detective Needles should be here shortly. He said one of us needs to stay with you until he arrives."

That made me feel better. My breathing had finally returned to normal, my heart no longer felt like it was natives from a foreign country jumping up and down and hearing the beat of a different drummer, and my thoughts were starting to make sense...well, at least to me.

At this point, I didn't care about what anyone else thought.

I was thinking about what Mickey had said earlier. Dear old dad was trying to rattle my self-confidence by declaring he wasn't my real dad. Even though he had caught me off guard by saying that I had seen my birth certificate, and his name was on there as my dad. Was it possible he really wasn't my biological dad? Yes, of course. Did I believe I was his daughter although I didn't see any family resemblance? Yes, I did. Do I think my mother would have told me if someone else was my father? Yes, I did. Good lord, the woman told me way more than I ever wanted to know about anything and everything growing up. I didn't think she had harbored any secrets about my paternity identity.

Sam walked through the door. "Is there any place in this town where you're going to be safe?"

He said it jokingly. I burst into tears.

Chapter 12

Apparently, my whole psyche was in worse shape than I thought. Wiping the sudden onslaught of tears with the heels of my hands, I muttered, "I'm sorry" several times.

Sam nodded at the officer. "It's okay, I've got it from here."

Turning back to me after the officer left, Sam suggested, "I can see that you need food. Let's go to Huddle House."

With a cheesy grin, he said, "Um, Harper, I think you need to put some clothes on.

They're probably not going to let you in there wearing just a nightgown."

I sniffled and nodded. I was also mortified. I hadn't really paid any attention to the fact that I was in my nightgown after my shower. My modesty level had been derailed by seeing Mickey in my room.

A few minutes later after being served hot coffee at the Huddle House, yes I had changed into jeans and a tee shirt, I glanced up at Sam. "Do you have any idea what's going on here? I'm getting tired of dead bodies showing up near me."

Trying to make a joke, I semi-laughed, "Is there something in the water that's causing this?"

Sam's brown eyes twinkled, his dimple deepened, he chuckled, "I'm wondering the same thing, Harper."

"What's up with Mickey? What happened to the box and Fat Freddy?" I involuntarily shuddered at thinking of Fat Freddy.

Sam leaned back in the booth, draping an arm on the back. "I can't tell you everything yet, Harper, but I can tell you that you have helped law enforcement tremendously."

He nodded at the waitress for more coffee. "The box left Duval County and made its way into our county. Once it did that, we could arrest whoever had the box. There are some legal technicalities involved but we did everything by the book. I'm sure you noticed the police cars zooming past you last night."

I nodded while taking a sip of the steaming hot coffee.

"Those were our guys en route."

Interrupting him, I asked, "But what about the flashing lights? Wouldn't that warn them?"

Sam chuckled again. "If they, or anyone, hadn't done anything wrong, they would have slowed down or pulled off to the side of the road to let us pass.

"In this case, we were hoping they would take off speeding, which is exactly what they did. Here's what is interesting. There were two cars hightailing it down the road."

"Wow! That means..."

"Yes, they were both carrying several boxes that field-tested for cocaine.

Those boxes are worth hundreds of thousands of dollars on the street."

I just sat there stunned. Poking at my corned beef hash and eggs, I asked, "Do you think it's safe for me to go back home now? I mean, you've got Mickey and, I guess, all of the other guys. I should be safe, right?"

Was I nervous? Yes, of course. What if the sniper hadn't been caught? Was my life still on the line, so to speak? I really wanted to go walk on the beach for solitude. I wanted my soul to be nourished by the waves gently rolling in and splashing the salty water on my feet. I wanted to walk in the water and have all my troubles washed away.

But fear seemed to have fallen on me like an old nasty coat I wanted to be rid of but couldn't make myself throw away because it held too many memories. If I threw away the old coat, would that mean all my memories ceased to exist? Was that a risk I wanted to take? I didn't know. I did want to be free of the fear.

"Harper," Sam's voice was soft, "you can go home, and you'll be safe. The cleaning lady is supposed to come around ten this morning. You can go back to the hotel and sleep or read or watch tv if you want."

Nodding, curling up in hotel soft bedding sounded incredibly enticing, "Sure. I'm ready to go whenever you are."

Back in the hotel room, I didn't bother exchanging my clothes for my nightgown. I simply crawled in bed and pulled the covers over my head. Right before

I dozed off, it occurred to me that Sigmund Freud would have a field day with my actions; and, more than likely, turning me into a victim of everything that had happened. I didn't care. Why do these weird thoughts invade my brain at the oddest times? I fell asleep.

Waking up a very relaxing six hours later, I actually felt refreshed and decided to go home.

Sam's cleaning lady was finishing up when I arrived. My apartment looked better than when I first moved in. I tried asking her questions about Sam...like how long she had known him and how long she had worked for him. I received a smile from her. Thinking maybe she spoke only Spanish, I asked, "Hablas ingles?"

She laughed. "Yes, of course, I speak English. It's just that the answers to your questions are confidential. I don't know how Sam would like me to answer them. So..." She spread open her arms slightly with her palms up.

Smiling, I agreed. "Gotcha. Honestly, it's none of my business either. I was just trying to be friendly."

Waving at the clean living room, "This is fantastic! You did a great job of cleaning up all the glass. How much do I owe you?"

I was reaching in my purse for my wallet. Yes, I still carry cash although it wouldn't have surprised me if she had said Venmo or Paypal would be acceptable methods of payment.

"Nothing." She was still smiling. Okay, did this mean Sam was going to expect a 'friends with benefits' thing from me? He was cute but I wasn't sure if I was ready for that yet.

"Um, did he pay you and I reimburse him or how does this work?" I was confused.

She picked up all her cleaning supplies and headed for the door. "Ask Sam."

The plate glass window had been replaced, the apartment was clean, and I saw a note on the counter. Picking it up, "Meet me at the steakhouse at five tonight. Sam."

CHAPTER 13

I arrived first and got us a table. Deciding to spruce up a bit, I was wearing dark blue slacks, a white blouse, and a red necklace, just big enough to be seen but not ostentatiously huge where it took over my whole outfit.

"You look nice." Sam slid into the red faux leather booth seat. "Special occasion?"

I grinned back. "Maybe. I'm hoping you can tell me more details on Mickey and the drug bust."

The waitress came by, and Sam ordered for the two of us. Normally, I'm not wild about men ordering my food, however, since I've now shared several meals with him, he knew what I liked. I always ordered the same thing.

Taking a sip of iced tea, he nodded. "Yes, now I can tell you everything. The Times Union is going to have a big article on us tomorrow. The news stations are going to have some coverage tonight on their ten and eleven o'clock newscast. This may even make the national news."

I raised my eyebrows. "Really?"

"Mickey played in a band for years and after digging into his background a little bit more, we discovered there was a somewhat surprising connection between the bars or clubs that he played in and how it was always a military town."

"And, let me guess, the clubs were relatively near a base." I grinned, "He was either running drugs or connecting with people who were."

Sam touched the end of his nose. "Bingo! He was actually the connector. He would find a guy, usually an officer who had just returned from an overseas deployment, and then tell this officer that his buddy was killed in action. He had received a box from him right after he was killed. His buddy had told him if anything happened to him, this box needed to go to a specific person on base. How could he find this individual and, more importantly, how could he get the box to him?"

He took a sip of his iced tea. "Here's the kicker, most of the officers would take the box and have it delivered to the guy on base."

"They didn't know they were aiding and abetting someone in a felony crime, right?" I was almost bouncing up and down in the booth. "That's wild!"

Sam agreed. "Yes, even though the military warns about such scams, it's still very easy to pull off. Since Mickey was a musician, he often found an officer who knew how to play a little guitar or who could sing and would offer to let the guy play or sing a song or two on stage in exchange for delivering the box."

"It fulfilled a dream of the officer to play in a band on stage, right?" I grinned. "I'm betting the officer had a couple of drinks under his belt and his guard was down."

"Probably. Mickey also gave them some song-and-dance about getting injured and getting out on a medical discharge. So, he was a brother in arms to these guys."

"Was he ever in the military?" I was chowing down on my steak. I didn't realize how hungry I was.

"Not that we can find. The FBI ran Mickey through their database and, surprisingly, nothing ever showed up on him except those drunk and disorderly charges I told you about earlier. No speeding tickets, no military background, nothing."

Swallowing, "I wondered if he was on their payroll somewhere along on the line."

"Nope."

"Did any of his band members know what he was doing? It seems a little odd that he could have been doing this for years and not gotten caught."

He finished chewing before answering. "Apparently, Mickey's only been doing this for about three or four years."

He held up his hand to keep me from interrupting. "Mickey lost a lot of money, according to him, on the Super Bowl. He was offered the opportunity to work his debt off by delivering boxes to the various clubs in different military towns.

"Mickey's singing like a bird and has admitted that his drug of choice is alcohol and smoking a little weed here or there. He wasn't into coke, which made him a safe bet as far as delivering it."

Pushing back my now empty plate, "So, basically, he was just the mule delivering packages? How did this all end up with Mason being murdered and me being shot at? I still haven't figured that part out yet."

"Crème brûlée?"

This was a man after my own heart! My favorite dessert ever. I nodded my approval. My little fat cells were jumping up and down in sheer happiness. He signaled for two of them to the waitress.

"Kind of a sad thing about Mason..."

I snorted, "Other than the fact he died you mean."

Sam smiled, "Well, there's that. Mason played in the band with Mickey..."

"So, he really was my half-brother?" I was still curious about that.

"Yes. Anyway, Mason played drums in the band off and on for Mickey. The box was given to him by accident. The label said M. Rogers and Mason thought it was for him. He opened the box, discovered the coke, and had a major fight with Mickey. He threatened to go to the police. Mickey, of course, couldn't allow him to do that. Mason got mad and left."

"He went to the beach to think things through," I guessed. "After Mickey was his dad and he was probably struggling with whether to turn him in or not."

Sam nodded, "That's what we think. Mickey panicked, thinking Mason was going to turn him in. He called..."

"Fat Freddy!" we said in unison and gave each other high fives just as the waitress placed our desserts in front of us.

"I've seen people get excited before about crème brûlée but never to the point of high fives," she laughed.

"It's a long story," Sam winked at her.

I gently tapped my spoon on the hardened sugar top and scooped up a mouthful of the delicious custard. I sure hoped this dessert was on the menu in heaven.

"Is Fat Freddy the mastermind behind all of this?" I asked.

"I don't think so," Sam paused for a moment and then continued, "Fat Freddy was controlling Mickey and when Mickey had any problems, he called Fat Freddy to handle it."

Starting to laugh, I sputtered out, "Dear old dad is a chicken!"

Sam nodded, "Pretty much. We know he called Fat Freddy about Mason. We strongly suspect he's the one who had the sniper kill Mason. We can't one hundred percent prove that though."

Holding up my spoon, "Wait! Who owned the condo where the sniper shot from? Is there any connection there?"

Shaking his head again, "Older couple from Miami own it and they were on a cruise."

"But those places have security and..."

"And people hire moving companies all the time to move their furniture in and out. He very easily could have had access to their floor that way.

"Regardless, whoever he was, he didn't leave any incriminating evidence. We're not sure who he is."

With that last statement, all the delicious food I had eaten dropped down to my feet. Fear threatened to crawl up my legs and back into my body.

"What do you mean, 'you don't know who he is'?" I almost screeched.

Sam put his hands out signaling me to keep the noise level down. This wasn't his life we're talking about! Okay, he's a police officer and his life is on the line every day but he chose to do that. I, on the other hand, did not choose to be a target for anyone.

"Is he black ops?" I was still a wee bit too loud.

Sam frowned at me. "Do you mind keeping it down a little? The whole world doesn't need to know this yet."

I glared at him. "It's not your life we're talking about!"

"Harper," he was struggling to stay patient, "do you want to hear the rest or do you want to call it a night?"

I scrunched up my face. Details, I wanted to know more details. "Go ahead."

He almost gave me an eye roll. "Once Mason realized what was in the box, he packaged it back up and had it delivered to you. Before you even ask, Mickey had your address. No, I don't know how he had it, but he did. I guess Mason thought you knew what was going on and that's why he had your name on the paper in his hand when he was killed."

"In other words," I almost whispered, "I'm safe."

Smiling, Sam nodded. "Yes, because you did just what you were supposed to do. You delivered it and left."

"Because I put the tracking device in the truck that's how you knew when Fat Freddy left Duval County and entered ours."

"Bingo."

"So, Sam, if they hadn't panicked, they would have gotten away with coke?"

He touched the end of his nose. He hadn't finished eating his dessert yet and I wondered if I might get that last spoonful. Sam must like me because he pushed the ramekin over to me. "There you go. But, yes, they probably would have been able to continue their little game."

He wiped his mouth. "Mickey sang like a canary when we arrested him. Fat Freddy and his buddy refuse to answer any questions, including their names, and they've already lawyered up."

I just nodded. "One last question, Sam. You said you thought you recognized the sniper's voice on the phone. Did you ever remember who it was?"

He smiled, "I guess I was wrong."

I wasn't sure I believed him but I didn't think he'd tell me.

Taking another sip of his tea, "So, you see, you helped us to make a big drug bust." Sam leaned back in the booth. "You should be proud of yourself."

Strangely, I wasn't. I couldn't really verbalize it. I still had a niggling feeling something was off. Maybe I should talk to Ronnie about everything.

CHAPTER 14

You have got to be kidding me!" squealed Ronnie. "Harper, girl, nobody but NOBODY would ever believe this story!"

He held up the newspaper with the bold headline of "Murder at Jax Beach!"

"A lot of the good stuff didn't even make the paper! I love it!"

I laughed. It had only been a couple of days since the news broke about Mickey, the drugs, the arrests, and I had been interviewed on several national tv shows.

My book sales were better than they had ever been.

Sitting in the pet store, sipping coffee with my dear, sweet friend, it suddenly occurred to me that moving back to Palm Park hadn't been such a bad idea after all. My hometown was starting to grow on me in a good way. Maybe that's all it took, moving away for a number of years and then coming back. Maybe Thomas Wolf was wrong...you can go home again...but with a different perspective. Letting go of old baggage wasn't such a bad thing.

Ronnie handed me the most darling little Maltese puppy. "She needs you to love on her."

I nuzzled the soft, curly hair on her tiny little head. "Ronnie, you know what's really odd?"

"What, honey?"

"Fat Freddy and his buddy disappeared with the FBI."

Ronnie chuckled, "Well, you know what they say...politics makes strange bedfellows."

Nodding, I said, "I love my country, it's the government I fear. I doubt we'll ever know the truth about what really happened. Who knows? All of this may be helping to fund some secret boogity-boogity government covert program."

"Who cares? You're safe, honey, and you can bring me coffee whenever you want!" Ronnie held up a puppy for me to pat.

"Okay, girl, no more murders. At least not in Palm Park or Jacksonville."

"Well, there's always St. Augustine."

We laughed.

MURDER AT PALM PARK - CHAPTER 1

Sarah was slumped over the table, her coffee with an obscene amount of liquid sugar in it was dripping off the edge, so was red fluid. The new barista, well, let's just say he wasn't going to be making any coffee drinks ever again.

I threw up as I was punching nine-one-one. My hand was shaking so badly that I now only had about half a cup of coffee left. I was now wearing the rest of it on my hand, arm, and the front of my shirt.

While waiting for the police to show up, it was only minutes but felt like hours, my thoughts dive-bombed my psyche.

I am a highly paid escort. I am young, cute, and deadly. I am an assassin.

No, no. That's not right. I am an opera singer. Yes, that's it. I open my mouth and beautiful, lyrical notes grace the air in the theatre.

I am a professional liar, and I am paid very well for it. What am I? I could be an actor, an attorney, in sales or advertising, a detective, or a writer.

"Seriously! Get out of your head. I can see story ideas bouncing around in your brain." Sarah had grumped at me. We've been friends since before breakfast. Actually, we've known each other since the fourth grade. We are not best friends...just good friends who know way too much about each other in certain areas of our lives. Still, when Sarah's not craving something to eat every two or three hours, she can be a lot of fun.

"What's wrong with you?" I grinned. It was just so much fun to see how much I could annoy Sarah, especially when I knew she was skating on the edge of crazy without her morning caffeine and sugar fix.

She grabbed her cup of coffee from the new barista at Coffee & Cupcakes, took a sip, put it back on the counter, and pushed it back to him. "It doesn't have enough sugar in it. I specifically asked for six shots. You didn't do that."

The guy inhaled deeply through his nose, letting the air out slowly through his nostrils, "Do you want me to put more in this cup or do you want a new one?"

Sarah snapped, "What do you think?"

"Hey, Sarah, chill." I held up three fingers to the guy. "Just put that many in the cup."

She started to say something, and I decided to shut her down. "Stop it! Tip the man."

Glaring at me, she snatched the mug that now had more sugar in it than our ancestors had had in a year, "No!"

Deciding our friendship probably needed a break, a long break, I tipped the young man. Taking my coffee and ignoring Sarah seated at one of the little tables, I started for the door.

"Hey!"

I ignored her and kept walking.

Looking back on it, I was amazed at how unobservant I was...or, just call it being too self-absorbed with Sarah's bad manners that I wasn't paying attention to the tall individual coming through the door. I was already out on the sidewalk trying to decide if I was going home to start writing a new story or if I was going to go pet the new puppies at Ronnie's pet store when I heard two double shots.

It took a moment for it to register that those were gunshots that I heard. Behind me. In the coffee shop.

Turning around, I rushed through the door. I don't know that I was thinking anything when I entered the store. My brain stops having coherent thoughts when I'm scared.

That's when I saw Sarah and called the cops.

Detective Sam Needles, really that is his name, walked over to where I was now sitting inside the store. "Please tell me you're not rehearsing a scene for a new book or something."

I shook my head. There was a small, unfortunate incident that had happened several months earlier when several mothers at the local park had observed me, Ronnie, Sarah, and Ruthie acting out a scene for a new book, thought we were trying to kill each other, and called the cops. We were but it was because I was trying to figure out the action details and how to describe it in a chapter. I'm a visual person and I needed to see a person's movement before I could write it.

Sam had been dispatched because the local patrol officers were off getting coffee and donuts or something.

Let's just say he wasn't amused when I told him those nosy mothers should have been paying more attention to their precious little progenies rather than adults on the other side of a public park who were minding their own business.

I told him what had happened.

"Was it a man or a woman coming through the door as you were going out?"

I shrugged. "I think it was probably a man because he was so much taller than I am."

Sam tried to keep from snorting. "You do realize you're only about five-three on a good day."

Huffing and trying to stand taller, there's only so much vertical height I can do even with taking deep breaths and blowing it out. "I'll have you know I'm five-four. Don't make me any shorter than I already am."

"So, the person was tall. What were they wearing? Did they have anything in their hand? Hair color or where they wearing a hat? Can you describe anything about this individual?"

Shaking my head, I said, "Um, I was kinda not paying attention. I was irritated with

Sarah's poor manners with the new guy, the new barista."

Sam nodded his head. "Did Sarah have any enemies? Anyone she was having a problem with? Owed money to?"

I suddenly realized how little of Sarah's personal life I actually knew. When we got together, all we did was talk about everyday things, nothing important, and nothing really personal.

"Sarah was dating or, rather, had gone out on a coffee date with a guy she met online. But I don't know anything about him."

I hadn't been wild about her picking men out of a lineup on a dating website and told her so. I didn't know the guy's name or anything about him. She told me I was an old fuddy-dud. Seriously? Who even uses words like that anymore? We had exchanged unpleasant words and today was the first day we had seen each other in a week.

With her being so snarky at the barista, I hadn't even cared enough to stay and ask her what was wrong. Maybe my sub-conscious had picked up bad vibes or maybe it was just me deciding that I'd had enough of her negativity. Whatever it was, I didn't want it in my life.

Maybe I should feel badly about my thoughts and feelings but, to be honest, I really didn't. I was sad she was dead, had been murdered, but I wasn't freak-ing out about it. My throwing up was more about seeing blood than anything else. I have a notoriously weak stom-ach when it comes to seeing body fluids, even seeing a kid spit on the ground can cause me to want to vomit. Go figure.

No expression on Sam's face. "Thought you had been friends for years. How could you not know who she was dating?"

Did I dare say we didn't have that type of relationship because that wouldn't make sense...or maybe it did. Just because we were women and friends for years didn't mean we shared all the details of our lives. Or, at least, I don't.

To share all details, intimate details, of my life involved a level of trust that I just simply do not have for most humans. Dogs, yes; humans, no.

Also, I must admit, I truly wasn't that interested in who Sarah was dating right now. Since my own dating life was minimal...who am I kidding? It's non-existent, which means, I wasn't remotely interested in who she was dating. It was different when we were both dating someone because then we had things to talk about but with me not having anyone in the romance department at the moment, I didn't care.

I wasn't sure how to respond to Sam's question, so I shrugged.

To read the rest of MURDER AT PALM PARK, get it at your favorite retailer.

About the Author

I grew up in Palatka, Florida, traveled the Southeast extensively for a number of years, and now make my home in Jacksonville, Florida where I am in the friends witness protection program due to past associations in Palatka. Some folks just don't have a sense of humor.

To join my VIP Newsletter and to receive a FREE book, go to www.SharonEBuck.com/newsletter.

I absolutely love readers because without you I'd be eating peanut butter and crackers. I greatly appreciate you and your support.

People are always asking if I'm available for speaking engagements. The short answer is "Yes, of course." In fact, I can even do a Zoom event for your book club.

Would you be kind enough to recommend this book and share the laughter with your friends? I appreciate it!

Thank you for being a loyal fan!

ACKNOWLEDGEMENTS

Thank you to my wonderful support team and friends for your encouragement, words of reassurance, inspiration, and belief in me on those days when the blank computer screen would stare back at me like a one-eyed monster daring me not to write anything. I survived and conquered.

In no special order, thanks to the following individuals:

Kim Steadman – There should be a law about how much we're allowed to laugh on the phone. Thankfully, there's not. Thank you for your friendship and the time we spend talking about writing, books, the book business, and just chatting. Visit KimSteadman.com

Michelle Margiotta – Your music has lifted me up when I was frustrated with my writing process, when I had doubts, and it has nurtured the very depths of my soul. Your music is so filled with colors and swirls dancing throughout your compositions that one cannot help but to be totally enthralled and inspired by your incredible gift. Visit MichelleMargiotta.com

Cindy Marvin – my friend and attorney who tries (hard) to keep me out of trouble before I even get into it.

McDonald's Baymeadows @ I-95, Jacksonville, FL - Keisha and her morning crew for serving me vanilla iced coffee every morning. They jumpstart my day with their smiling faces. It's how I start my day.

Southside Chick-Fil-A in Jacksonville, FL – Patty, the awesome marketing manager, and her team who have hooked me on frosted coffee. I am now an addict LOL Every fast-food restaurant in America should take lessons on customer service from them. It's always a delight to go into a happy place of business. I am always treated like a friend, not a customer.

George and Mama at Athenian Owl Restaurant on Baymeadows in Jacksonville, FL –My favorite Greek restaurant and they make me feel at home every time I eat there.

And, lastly, thank you to all my loyal readers and fans. I love and appreciate you!

To God be the glory.

Purchase my books at your favorite retailer

Book 1

A Dose of Nice and Murder

Book 2

A Honky Tonk Night and Murder

Book 3

The Faberge Easter Egg and Murder

Book 4

Little Candy Hearts and Murder

Book 5

Lights, Action, Camera and Murder

Book 6

A Turkey Parade and Murder

Book 7

Cookies and Murder

Book 8

Flamingos and Murder

Book 9

Bowling and Murder

Purchase my books at your favorite retailer

101
Summer
Jobs for
Teachers

Kids Fun
Activity
Book

Counting
Laughs

Made in the USA
Columbia, SC
21 January 2025

52209878R00124